Don't worry
I am here

Kaushiki Prasad

pencil

ISBN 978-93-5610-344-3
© Kaushiki Prasad 2022
Published in India 2022 by Pencil

A brand of

One Point Six Technologies Pvt. Ltd.
123, Building J2, Shram Seva Premises,
Wadala Truck Terminal, Wadala (E)
Mumbai 400037, Maharashtra, INDIA
E connect@thepencilapp.com
W www.thepencilapp.com

DISCLAIMER: *This is a work of fiction. Names, characters, places, events and incidents are the products of the author's imagination. The opinions expressed in this book do not seek to reflect the views of the Publisher.*

Author biography

I am an author and artist

CONTENTS

1 5

1

1

Lately, I was thinking if my parents can live without me or not? Won't it destroy my brother? But it hurts so bad I can't handle anything. I am tired of hearing to the people, hearing to all those words. I was planning to end my life and then I ended up writing a note in an app hidden under everything. No one knows about it.

Here is how it goes .....
" I was going through a lot lately. Rather I have no one who can understand me. My brother, I know he will hear me speak but I don't dare to do so. I don't want to stress him up. I don't know what I feel anymore and I don't think anyone even cares. I can't handle my pain, my feelings. I am tired of the fight. A fight I have to do with myself every day to survive. Is there anything I can do? Please say me! I want to ask someone, talk to someone, is there anyone who can speak to me? I know you all are ready to but I am somehow scared to bother you, always thinking I am annoying you by speaking about the same depressing things again and again. I want to destroy that part of me but it seems inseparable, I can only get rid of it by ending my life because there's no end to it. It is just not one reason which beholds but there are many I can't

express. Many people I can blame but I don't want to because they don't have any part to play with my death or my depression. My name doesn't matter anymore, it's just a form of a word. The name someone else chose it and that's gonna carve on the marble stone on my grave. Nothing matters anymore, it's just that I tried to be happy and I failed to do so and here I am ending my life in a sad gloomy moment I might leave behind.

I would finally say I loved you all even you didn't, thank you for everything."

Let me tell you guys my story. I am Kevin ..... Kevin Watson Kanye. I live in Winnipeg, which is in Canada. I was actually from a small place in Africa. Yes, you may never have heard of this place. My parents who are were from California but they worked as social workers. That's how they met each other, married for 21 years by now long story to be told. I was 3 when they decided to move back to the USA but they got jobs in Canada. People back there, in Africa usually slaughtered and murdered whites because they think whites may enslave them again. We were one of those whites who were in danger so they decided to leave the place. Not everyone was bad there, my parents have many good friends too who didn't wish them to leave but everything was out of hand by then.

Now I am 17, I have a three years younger brother, he was born after we moved to Canada, I don't know anything about that place anymore, I don't care either and my parents never wish to speak about it. Both of them do a normal job now. Normal life, normal people. There was nothing to describe anything but who doesn't have problems? My life was the most boring of them, it was just a circle, the same things happen again and again. I have no friends, I think but I do ..... Sometimes don't want to talk to anyone but I want to... I am weird I know, I don't even utter a word to my neighbor never spoke a word to them because I never wanted to but I was completely different at school......kinda.I was so friendly to everyone, everyone was good to me so was I, it was like I have so many friends but the truth was I didn't. Giving a wave back when they waved at me, saying byes and they asking me how I was and saying I was fine and asking the same question and getting the same boring reply does not describe a friend, never. It was just Radom people I know, that's it. Talking about my class of course the best one of all. We were same or being together since year made us so, all were friends to each other so was I close to them......everyone.....that's how I think, each of them. Rather in reality everyone has their groups whom they were close to the most spend most of the time with and I feel that I am interrupting them because my words didn't reach their ears whenever I said a word, they usually speak in French, I understood them but I had trouble speaking so they always talked to me in English but still I can't handle things. I am tired of not being heard, people not hearing me most of the time.....feeling like a ghost became an obvious thing to me, everything was just a piece of shit so was I . Truly speaking they were good they try to speak to me even many times, not talking to their friends rather, of course, they talk to me in English, yes they know the language though. Yet like I am always the second choice for them, it wasn't that they were bad but things still bothered me a lot. They were kind, caring, appreciating everything, encouraging me a lot with my drawings, writings, and everything I do they said I was multi-talented but I have so less self-confidence I trusted no one, even a point they liked me. My two friends Peter and Peggy were really good ones but like always they had closer mutuals, I constantly think they like me Or not? Peter thinks I am really funny but once was rude to him. Peggy thinks I am funny and depressed I know nothing about myself anymore, I think I am a piece of shit, who doesn't speak about his feelings. Everyone has a different opinion about me especially me being a lot confused and I don't know what's mine. Sometimes I show them my works they unsee it not intensely but they do, sometimes my words don't reach their deaf ears so I pretend nothing happened, they still care about me but that wasn't the truth it was something bad .....something going on in my head. I always lay in bed wondering what was my fault, was it being born? Being a burden on my parents, being useless. I always questioned my existence.

I always scored average grades, I wasn't good at sports either, my parents wanted me to be perfect in everything but I wasn't. I always want to cry about things but I can't, I just pretend to be happy even I am emotionally broken into pieces, faking a smile wasn't easy, all of it feels so cold, but I wanted the sunshine, bright days, but it was different it was cold, snowy, freezing no light of hope, nothing. Wished I can die but then I think how did my parents and brother goanna live without me? Although I felt everything they still love me, They were just the reason I was still alive. I love spending time with my parents my brother and I wanted no one else... I think and even sometimes not. My parents were disappointed with me because of my behavior, of course, because they cared. I was almost 18 but can't go shopping alone, I always insisted my brother come with me because I didn't want to talk to the cashier. Yes, I was that bad at it. My parents even tried to change me but they don't understand that it takes time and they are not ready to understand that, somehow I think they were the cause of my problems.....many reasons lie ahead.....

Nothing's gonna work till you work on yourself and I wasn't interested because I thought it was a waste of time. Everyone has their friends group and I had none, I felt bad, and then I wanted no one to.

I always thought my brother is favorite child to my parents because he was active, easily can interact with anyone around, help them with courses, had many friends, scored good grades, was good at sports, was a good writer, he was multitalented. Then it was me who was useless can't do anything. Still being grateful to have such a brother, who spends most of the time with me rather than his friends because he always knew what I was going through. Sometimes I want to be him and then I cry, my jealousy always make me yell at him, I don't but still I do.

Both my parents worked they didn't even have time to eat dinner together, it was just weekends or holidays we can, still, it was the best time but sometimes things aren't the way it is.......

2

I was sitting in my room at my table looking out the window straight forward there was a house that had invisible people in it because I have never seen any of them even it's been three months already. I was alone and of course, my room was a messed up thing and I was lazy enough to clean it by myself...... I was supposed to study but instead, I was talking to my online friends. I have many good ones Steve, Vale, Daniela, Leigh, Aaron and many more ..... All were kind supportive, nice like my classmates, was always ready to help me, understand me, take out the in me but Yes like reality sometimes I feel ghosted like with my friends.

(Not specifically pointing out people, truly I feel with everyone and every time.) They say, (some people)they would see my stuff and sometimes they don't. It feels so stupid of me..... Truly anxiety kills you from inside so am I killing myself. I know they have their works, busy with things but it hurts that they promise you to see your works and then they don't or they don't say how it is. It feels you have made the most shitty thing on this planet and no one is interested to look towards it.....

Sometimes you want them to be honest with things but again you can't handle the truth because you are losing it. You want some motivation that you get from their kind words, sometimes which is hard to believe in. I hate myself so much that I can't trust myself anymore or any good others say about me, Daniel says that I shouldn't be underestimating myself, I should believe in myself more in my works but I can't because little things that happened in past made me think I am crap, I know I should move on, do those words even matter? No, right but still I can't.....can't move on from hating myself and working more on loving myself, caring about myself a little more. No, I can't. You guys don't know how much I hate myself.....all I do is hurt myself mentally and physically by hitting my foot on something hard or punching against the wall till my hands get burning red or bleeds, I try to cut my hands from any sharp object near me. or sometimes I break pens and many more things I do and it gives me nothing.

I don't trust anyone when they say my work is amazing or I am amazing, I am not annoying and can't stop thinking that. No matter how much Steve or Hellen taught me. I don't listen to them and it makes me hate myself even more and every single thing that happens to me in my life everything does make me hate myself. Each day it's a start of something new, the start of getting a new reason to hate me and kill me in pieces, there would be a million words if I start and there's no end to my anxiety. I have self-diagnosed myself as having anxiety or depression having all the possible symptoms. It has made me think I am going through it but what if I am not and I shouldn't be doing this? I can't consult a doctor because saying my parents about it will be hard, they think a child cannot go through depression even a 20-year-old can't have problems but the problem is they don't understand anyone else's problem except theirs so I can't speak about it all they will say is I am sad. Here's one of my shitty works you decide should I hate me or not about this?

Sometimes I wish I can leave this world. I think it's not gonna matter to anyone if I leave. Will anyone be sad? Or unhappy? Does anyone care if I am here or not? Does it matter if I am there? Does anyone even want me with them or I am just a burden?

Or It's only for a day or two they will cry, they will moran on my leave and soon my memories will be blurry and I will be forgotten slowly, just that my name will stand on my grave and it will be forgotten away from that very day. I wouldn't be remembered, I won't have anyone visiting my place? Does anyone even care?

(Just for no reason I wrote it in my loneliness, I know, it's nobody reading it. Because if there was anyone why will I even write it?)

" Darkest is the shadows of pain
hidden underneath,
Thousands of tears that fleed away unnoticed,
Hundreds of nights spent picking up the pieces crying,
Stuck in the deepest of the ocean,
Yet drowning in search of light,
Thus, trapped in the darkest of moments of life.
Long vanished happiness never to
be refined,
Feels like a ghost trying to find a way to live a life.
Till waiting to see a rainbow in the sky after a stormy night.
"

I have no words regarding this so……

(Same day a few moments later).

It was Saturday and my mom had a holiday. We decided to go someplace today but my dad got some work at the last moment. It always happens not a new thing but I am tired of it.

I got a call from my mom downstairs
" Kevin come and get your snacks ".
She doesn't usually call out this way we go and grab it ourselves just because she is never at home at this time.
My brother Louis enters and as soon as he hears mom's word he stares at me in a way he wanted to know who will get the stuff. So I said " I will get 'em don't worry" Getting out off the table. I took a step down to the kitchen, guess what there was a cake and cookie dough. My brother liked cookie dough and I liked cakes, of course, the most amazing thing created on this planet I love them a lot any cake, I would love it but sometimes, some cakes taste gross. So I grabbed it in happiness, yes I can not always be depressed, I wasn't but who knows I get a breakdown and lock myself in a room for a week. Once I did for 3 weeks straight and my brother pulled me out of bed and we went on a walk, it was the best one I ever had. I am sometimes jealous of him. He is so good brother and I am a bad one. I do some things that make him feel sad but later he comes in giving me a warm hug.

I went up the stairs and from the top Louis was looking at me and I suddenly dropped his cookie dough, it was wrapped hopefully (hahaha). Seeing me dropping it he said " Bro you gotta find a way to not drop things " Actually I always drop things a lot. I am very clumsy. Once I dropped my mom's medicine which was in a nice glass-made container which as expected broke into many pieces. I thought I would get a kick shot for doing this but nothing happened, weird isn't it?

Louis and I sat down, now both of us were staring out of the window (quite a funny moment actually). So Louis

suddenly noticed at the window and was like
" Kevin, you look at that girl sitting right there she looks so weak, doesn't she? "
" Who," I asked (as I said earlier I have never seen anyone in that house but heard some stupid noises from there. It's not haunted actually, hahaha)
" Look at the balcony on the left side you see someone? "
" Oh yes, she. Looks like the wind is gonna blow her along, but it's not funny she is so weak honestly ".
" She is, you know why? " Louis asks looking at me
" I think she is sick but I won't conclude till I know anything "

" I think she is in your classmate"

"She is not or is she? "

" Ok, you don't know, seriously?"

He gave an exclamation

" Jeez save her, I feel bad, really bad"

" Me too " ......

We forgot about things started enjoying our evening snacks. Both of us love to share our food so half of the cookie dough went to me and half of my cake went to him. Sharing is the best thing but giving my sweet little brothers a little more is better. I will look at him with a smile when my heart is less filled with hate or sadness. Love you so much.......

3

Doubts

I love going out cycling with Louis. It's weird to hear this but I love to because anything I do with my brother is just a great experience. Whether it is hiking, skating, cycling, singing together without thinking how we sound or how loud we are, dancing to ear-burning music till our ankle breaks, it's all fun. I love doing everything with him, you can understand me. Not having him would have broken me into pieces.

So on such a fine Saturday evening, we were back after cycling for hours together. For the second most time I was seeing people in my neighbor's house. They were many, dressed in black. Like they were coming back from a funeral. Nothing doesn't seem good, moreover. Then Louis " What's wrong here? "
" I don't know either," I said
" Jeez...... " He said
" Let's go in, so who is doing the dishes? "
" Both of us" Louis "Great then "
(we gave a smile)

Mom was home already...
" So till where you went up to? "
" Who knows " Louis smiles and says. I was still thinking about what was going on outside so I asked...
" Mom, you know what's going on outside? "
" You mean in neighbors? "
" Yes," Louis and I said together.
" I am not sure a rumor says the girl who lived in the house passed away. They said she was sick "
" That 16-year-old girl? " Louis

" Yes," Mom, me " Who? "
" The girl we have seen a couple of days through window"
Louis
"Her! " I said in surprise because she was young and Yes I
was feeling really bad about it
" Kevin you need to step out of the house to know things
and you don't " Mom
" Yes," I whispered.
" Go clean up your selves both of you are untidy "
" Ok " Louis runs off but I was slowly taking steps in the
thought of the girl
" Are you ok Kevin? "
" Yes, ma" ......

Dad usually returns home late so we most of the time have
dinner without him. Sometimes mom doesn't come early
either so we(my brother and me) get the dinner ready, do
all the dishes,s, and go to sleep. It rarely we can get some
time to spend together.

An hour later we were at the dinner table it was late already
said so we started eating. It wasn't my favorite but I didn't
hate it either. I dropped my spoon as soon as I picked it up
to eat. Louis said " Bro one more time. " His words made
me laugh. I said after picking up the spoon " You find me
a way that I can stop using my phone. " " Using phone!
When did I say that? "Louis " Sorry, I mean dropping
stuff," I said.
" Find it yourself " Louis
" Thank you for your advice " I started laughing.

It was 10 pm already and dad did not come back. He has
given a call that he will be late today.

Louis and I were cleaning the table and was doing dishes. Mom has some work so we were helping her out.

While washing dishes

" Hey, you know anything about that girl next door? " Me
" Only that, her name was Margret, she was 16 and she passed away " Looks at me and continues "why? ".
" I don't know I feel bad for her "
" Me too" Louis
" I hope she can get the peace she was always seeking for,.here". I said
" Same here" Louis
" What! "
"Sorry" Louis.
" Come on do it quick, I want to sleep " Me
" I know it's Sunday tomorrow you won't get sleep early and wake up late or you will suddenly wake up and find it hard to fall asleep again. You won't be up before 10 am" Louis
" So true " I started laughing, so did he
" So what we can do today? "
" How about a movie or complete the series we were watching? "
" Great movie then!!! " Louis
" Which one? "
" IT from Stephen King " (he is crazy for Stephen King's)
" Ok "
I usually don't say what I want to do or what I think is good. My choices were never respected so I stopped making any. Now I find it so difficult to make very simple choices so I ask my brother sometimes... All the time.

Before going to bed we were looking for mom. We started seeking into her room she saw us. She asked " Everything's done "
" Yes, Yes, " Both of us said.
"Now what's your plan? "
" Movie " Louis
I thought mom was about to scold us but she didn't and said
" Ok no sound should come out"
" Ok ..... Ok " Both of us.

" Grab some popcorn and Netflix " Louis shouted in excitement
" Wait It's on prime video and we don't have any popcorns"
We started laughing again. It was good today we were happy, I was too but the girls were dead I can't stop thinking of it. Which was wearying me a lot.

He starts the movie and we started watching the movie. Then we heard some noise. It was the dad he was home, lately. We pushed the movie and their words were clear (mom and Dad's) they were fighting and yelling again. We can't do anything because sometimes when we try to stop them they yell at us and everything turns out shit. I was feeling so helpless. I suffer a lot because of their fights I don't want my brother to suffer too so I grabbed him in my arms. I know but I can't do anything just wait because I tried doing anything it was always a mess. I want to make sure my brother was ok. So both of them.......

It feels so helpless when you want to do something and you can't and the only thing that's left to do is to have regret for not doing anything, have the guilt of everything that happened, and blame yourself. That's what I do all the time.

My brother looks towards me and it was just " Don't worry, I am here "

4

Amy

Let me introduce myself.....ok, I am Amy Watson, I am an independent woman, works as a graphic designer,46 years old. Mother of two sons and I think it's the most difficult job on this planet.

My elder son is 17 years old and my younger son is 14. I am tired of my elder son's behavior because he is almost 18 and does so many things I don't understand. He is scared, fears a lot of things like public speaking, waiting for public speaking, I will be happy if he can speak to anyone straightforward He even fears dead a lot, I know everyone does but he does a lot, lot and gets a lot of panic attacks which he hides most of the time which weary me a lot. Last month his biology teacher gave me a call and said, Kevin got a heart stroke, I rushed to the school and took him to the hospital. Doctors said he got a panic attack, it happened when he was giving a presentation in his class. Why does he suffer a lot? He was just overthinking and got himself in this trap. He even fears loss, sometimes his teacher, talking to new people and so many things.

I am never gonna know how is he gonna survive in this world after all It's 2021! As expected 2020's lockdown was amazing to him, he enjoyed it like anything, he doesn't have to socialize, that's what made him happy of all but my younger son got frustrated because he can't go out. Hopefully, Kevin was there for him. I love to see how both are so supportive of each other, something is good.

My younger son is better on those points than my elder son. Kevin is insecure a lot about so many things but it doesn't mean Louis doesn't annoy or make me mad, I love them both equally but who will say it to Kevin.

My husband blame me for his conditions but he never cared for them, he was never there when we needed him. He was never.....

I scold my kids and sometimes I feel so bad after that and cried too. I have been married for the last 21 years to a man named Richard Kenley. I met him back in Africa. He was different back then so was I, young of course and many things changed since then. I don't know where to start from.

Flashback

I was 23, I was so passionate about so many things. I have dreams to do so many things, my admissions to achieve them. To do something for this world. Nothing of it included finding love in my life but life isn't like the picture you create in your head. It's something that you would never accept. So was it meeting Richard. Back in Africa, I use to work as a social worker but I even loved to draw that's how I became a graphic designer...... Thinking of those days makes me smile and even makes me go back and say to myself don't fall into this trap. Anyways time passed away and nothing can be changed now...... Where was I? Yes….. As always I was at work. Everyone said I was a good artist so I used to draw campaign posters back then. I was once doing the same, it was really hot there, the temperature was so high, I was sitting under a tent-like thing, sitting on a chair and a gentle-looking person appeared, he was firmly dressed, he looked gentle.

He said " Mam, your work is really beautiful, how did it come? "

" Thank you so much sir, it's for an upcoming campaign for kids" I replied.

" Don't call me sir, I am new here and even it seems you are senior here because I was sent to you" Richard

" Me? (in confusion I nodded my head) are you sure? " I asked

" Yes, mam. Aren't you Amy Watson? "He asked

" Then you are at the right place, I am Amy"
I replied.

" Hello then, I am Richard ……. Richard Kenley " He said

" Oh, hello Richard " Shakes hand

" Can I help you with something? " He continued

" Yes help me with this poster," I said. He agreed and sat beside me helping

He was such a kind person, I liked him that. I had just had a great day. It turned out he was an amazing artist too. He helped me a lot that day. (To be continued…..)

But now he doesn't draw anything and when Kevin draws a lot he scolds him. He has changed a lot. He doesn't care anymore and blames me. He is never there with us when we need him. Last year he was absent on Louis' birthday he waited a lot but Richard did not come. When he arrived it was already 12 and Louis slept getting mad at him. Kevin heard all the fight we had till the next 1 am, it's so depressing. He is so busy with his work that he doesn't have time for us?

A few months back when Kevin fell sick and then got himself hurt he did not come, saying he was busy. I alone need to take him to the hospital and get him back. He did not even pay a visit to him when Kevin got hospitalized for 2 days. He did not come. He has changed a lot. He does not love us anymore.

Yesterday it was Saturday finally we decided to go out for a family weekend trip. Guess what….. He again got some shot of fucking work and we stayed home. I am fucking frustrated with him. It was already late at night so we ate our dinner. Kevin and Louis completed doing dishes. I let them watch the movie because they were early waiting to go out since our trip was canceled, I can let them have a good time together. I was sitting in my room completing my leftover work. Then there was a noise someone was at the door. I went down to check-in. It was Richard. Time was already 11:30. I asked " Why Are you late today? "
He replied " Do you even care? "
I got mad at his reply. How can he say it?
" What do you mean. You are so late today, we were waiting for you all the time "

Richard
" You did? You and your kids have waited for me till dinner? No, right. Happily got yourself stuffed and was about to sleep"

Me
" What the fuck you mean my kids? Aren't they yours...It was getting late so….."

Richard
" So, without caring for your husband you ate. You know you made those fucking kids like you. Now I trust no more that they are my kids "

Amy (losing her temper)
" What the fuck! You are such bullshit I realized now. You can speak so bad of us like this and even judge my character like that? I am not one coming home late and canceling all family trips, it is you. I think you got yourself a new girlfriend, isn't it? "

Richard (starts yelling too)
" I come home for some peace and I get nothing, you are such nonsense, I shouldn't have come"

Amy (in the same tone)
" Go away. Why are you coming home then? Get yourself a new home, leave me and my kids alone, you don't think of us, our family anymore, right? You are just here to sleep and eat !"

Richard
" Ok, I am going, don't try to find me "

Amy
" Go, go to your girlfriend, I won't come back of you"

Richard
" You know what Amy I will go, you are gonna be such a wife I can never know. One more thing (points a finger to

her) I have no girlfriend, I think you are in a relationship, isn't it? "

Then Richard leaves banging the door hard. I was so hopeless and I can't understand his behavior anymore. He changed a lot since. I stayed up the whole night crying in bed. I don't want Kevin and Louis to hear me. It is so hard to be a mother and sometimes I find it hard to handle things. I wanted someone and I don't know who I should call it was so late and I was having a breakdown and I didn't have any friends. Even Richard left for nothing. Fuck my life……..

5

Been 4 years

Ever been on Instagram or Twitter? I have, it's already been 4 years. I met my first online friend on Twitter. She is from Indonesia, miles away from my place. I wish I can meet her one day. We even made a deal about cheesecakes and ramen (funny I know). I wanted to try some of it and she says Indonesia has the best of it. I don't know how I started following her but at first, I thought she is from far eastern countries, east Asia.

We had a lot of crazy conversations together. Although she is 8 years older we are great friends. She is amazing and eventually a great friend of mine. We have asked millions of questions about our likes and dislikes and she never judged it. Being a part of the small world makes you feel so different but when you come across many people you will find thousands of people like you and you won't feel alone or different but everyone has something bad to deal with, so does I.

Being a social media artist is hard but it did not bother me a lot at the start......On my birthday I drew James Gunn posted it and Damm!! He saw my drawing and shared it, things changed after that. Shane Grandes saw his story and I met a new friend from there. My followers increased, interaction and everything did. I met new people and so many things happened. I met Leigh, Steve, Hervé, Casey, Aaron, Daniel, Márcia, Vic, Kelly many more.....

Making a family was best of was inspired by chocolate (hahaha, sounds cute to me). It came out from a collaboration group made by my good friend. I met dozens of people there but with time many of them left, everyone got busy, and long day and night conversation came to an end. I didn't want to lose them but time blew away everything. I even made a triplet group with Cassey and Helen. Great time. Guess what's the worst part of it. I even wrote a poem on it (lol, yes). What am I even trying to say through this? Please help! I don't want to close them because they are the only people who speak to me and if I loo them then I will have no one. No one to talk to. Even online I will be lonely.

To be honest, rarely do people know about my anxiety because I don't speak about it till I feel comfortable. Talking to Steve always makes me feel good but then I also think. Why? Why do I speak about the same thing again and again? It's not like I don't want to speak about it but where on earth our conversation starts it will end at the same place
(sorry I find it funny ,) . Is he not tired of it? Am I not annoying him with all the conversation, after all, he is 10 years older, yes. He said he likes talking about life

conversations where we end every time. I like them too but what if I am getting back his anxiety and being a cause of it. I overthink a lot and I truly should give it a full stop, sorry. Am I just sharing my feelings rather than telling stories? Forgive me. The same happens when I talk to Hervé and Cassey.

Every time Daniel, Harvé, and Steve said to be happier, myself more but I can't…. Can't anymore. They say not to apologize a lot, if anyone wants to forgive you they will at once but I continue to do the same(kill me, I am saying everything in a good mood, don't judge me for that.) Daniel's words always make me so happy, he is good to all. I got close to him from one of his lives and eventually ate his brain (lol). Márcia, I don't want to make her mad let's say her Gustav….. Gustav Eiffel. She is crazy, good at creating crazy stories like Kinderss invasion everyone contributed to making such crazy and amazing story, Steve has amazing and beautiful ideas and has a great imagination. Daniel is a really good writer, his poems are something I admire a lot. If I start it will be an endless thing…..

Sometimes I wonder do they think of me as I do them? I don't want to lose any of them but being online becomes just a challenge, you can't interact with people and then nuclear Blasts in your head, all the storm, makes you
take a break and that break turns so peaceful that it feels so good you don't want to go back again. Even when you return no one cares that you vanished or they did but they feared to show their feelings? You can't judge anything anyway but still, anxiety makes you think of things you don't want to, every bad thing which can take place comes

to your head. Everyone is really good and supportive though and loving.
Fuck the anxiety!!!!!!!

"Days I passed by talking to those I never thought would end up at this point,
Things I regret to refine, everything blew away with the wind.
To those I loved infinite,
now are like those strangers I have ever seen.
In those woods we were once lost,
talking day and night till the moment ceased like the morning mist after the sun is high.
Now are like the deserted land where lives have never been.
Once been inseparable like the stars behold in the sky, flowers in the field, trees touching the yonder light.
Now are just something which was never in life.
Felt the pride to be theirs' but at once lost all of them.
Now just the sweetest memories behold in the heart like the rainbow in the sky.
Thus, would carry it along if I try, still can make me smile and can let tears fall from my eyes.... "

6

Ever given an examination which was about to decide your future, more likely a life and death situation. I know most of you did but I was about to. Of course was getting pressurized from teachers, parents, and everyone who can do it....

I use to sit at last in the corner. Some should sit at last and nobody gonna adjust so I did. In the morning we have chemistry class. What can be worse than a strict teacher? The principal was our chemistry teacher. She was quite experienced, for years she is handing the school and she does it so well.

I wish I can say to her about some bullies,who annoyed many of my classmates.

I usually sit at last but I don't know what was in my head I sat first. They with their gloomy-looking faces, with all the anger, pointed out to me, my heartbeat ridiculously raised. I was about to have a panic attack because of them, what are they doing here. I don't want to break out in front of everyone. They asked something and the moment my leg started shaking and I started taking deep breaths what….. I lost all my voice and they throws up all there frustration on me. I need to say what they were mad at before. Our biology teacher complained to our principal that they are missing the biology test and biology classes both of your our teachers scolded them for the next 40 minutes for being such annoying.

They asked me whether I was doing everything well or not, I said yes, and eventually, I scored a little more in my test. They doubted that I cheated, bullies here….. I hate it when someone doubts me for the wrong reasons. My parents always do that and them her. I was so mad at them and later I got to know all my classmates were mad at them too. Yes of course because our principal does things for right and they don't do it listen. It surprising that the complain went to their parents .Why don't these bullies understand that whatever teachers do are good for them sometimes? Do they have too many problems that ours is nothing? Since then I was feeling so bad. The next day in geography class I had a breakdown and I busted out in presence of my teacher it made no sense my friends who know my condition started making me feel better but I can't stop crying and was waiting for the class to end. Why do schools never teach us how to control mental health, how to overcome our fears, how to face our future problems, how to live our lives, how to make our career better. Wait how will they. These bullies just come to us and ruin our life why is there nobody who actually comes and say you good things. Then don't have a settled life how will they teach us? Instead of looking into their own life why they infrared with ours , they make it depressing. Sorry for being loud and miss using the language but I thought, is what I said.

After coming out of class in the same mood. Trying to handle myself. Some students from another class approach me and say
" Hey loser, what happened now? Did we do anything to you, baby? " They started laughing
Peter
" You shut yourself up or I won't leave you "

Bully
" Supporting this shit? You should be embarrassed to have him as a friend "

Peter
" You are no one to teach us who to be friends with and not, you know what….. Hopefully, we aren't your friends "

They got mad at his words and pushed him off. Some people from other classes approached and pushed them back.

One of them shouted
" Hey, what's wrong with you? "

" Leave them alone or you will pay a good price for this "
They left and I was having a storm in my head about the words they said and even they helping us, why did they?

One of them comes to me, her name was found to be Scarlet
" You are Kevin? "
I said " Yes, I am Kevin but I am not sure that the Kevin you are looking for is me. "

Scarlett
" Kevin Watson Kanye? "

I said
" Yes me "

" Come I want to know something from you, Peter you can some too"

I said " Me! You are sure? "
She looks meme disgustedly. We went out of the Hall and she began

" You know Margaret Woods? "

 I do not know about her
" Margaret Woods, sorry I don't "

Scarlett
" Your neighbor idiot "

" Yes … Yes I remember her, but I know nothing about her"

Scarlet
" It's fine if you don't, I just want you to help us "

I was confused
" Me? Why me? "

Scarlett
" Because I think she did not die of sickness, she committed suicide "

I was a little shocked
" What? What do you mean, how can you say that "

Scarlet
" You know nothing about her, right? See it's getting late now, we need your help. We will give you a complete explanation at the earliest but please try to understand things "

I am still confused
" Seriously? Ok, I will try to. I don't think I am a good person for help, I will still"

She
" Thank you but you are the right person or I won't be here. I will leave now I will talk to you about this on our trip. One more thing they said right you are so confused "

Me
" Who? "

She

"Our teachers"

My face so carped and I was like, what do? What do teachers say about me in this way? Why?

Peter was confused too so he asked
" What does she has to do with your neighbors?"

" I wonder, I guess Margaret was her friend" I replied

" I think so " Peter

I will hang out with Peter, I will stay at his house till evening because it was his birthday today. He even invited my brother. So we decided to go straight to his school. We have said it already to mom

(I was still thinking about a trip she said)

I asked
" What trip she was talking about? "

Peter

" You did not check the notice board? We are gonna have a trip to the USA "

" Wow!! That's amazing "

Peter

" If you don't come I will kick your ass"

(I started laughing)

" I will, even Louis will"

Peter

" Louis too, great! "

" Traitor, you like my brother more? "

Peter

" Yes " He cracked out then his friends entered and I became a ghost again (let's fake a smile)

It was really fun at a party. I really don't like taking pictures but my friend suggested so I took some of 'em. My brother enjoyed it a lot because he loves socializing, especially with my classmates. He is close.

7

So finally the day arrived, I was about to go to the USA. I was quite nervous but I can have some time together with my brother. Well fair enough and even I am gonna meet Harvé and Cassy. It will be my first time meeting online friends. I have already taken permission of cutting the trip in between and seeking somewhere else (hahaha). I am happy, something I was living for.

Our flight was about 1 hour 30 minutes long. I was fine on my fight. It's not my first time flying but my head loves to make scenarios about bad things. I can't help.

Finally, we were there. At the airport. There were people all around. It got a little warm when we departed. So we took off our jackets.

Some shouted from back to me " Kevin, Kevin. " I looked back it was Scarlett and Laura. Peter and Louis were with me. Peter said " And you say no one asks you"
I just looked at him, I wanted to say something but I wasn't able to.
" Kevin, I said we will talk about it in New York, "
" Yes, sorry I forgot. "
" No problem, I will catch up with you later. "
" Ok, Bye, " She said goodbye and left.
" Now to the hotel and never coming off of there. " Louis said. I started laughing no issue we will burst out.

We went to our hotel and it was really good. We got our room. Everyone needs to share the room with 3 people. So I Peter and Louis got into it.

I was watching them through the window. Most of the time and I noticed now crowed this place is. People everywhere. Anyways it was ok. I was even happy that I was having a good time with my brother. My mom called us often to check that we are doing alright. I think Louis got a call from dad too.

The next day we were about to go to some places first we went to Central Park Sightseeing Bike Tours – one of the most fun things to do in Central Park, Best of Brooklyn Walking Tour in Williamsburg which showcases the trendy areas of the Brooklyn borough, and more. Then we went to the 9/11 Memorial Museum. Studied about World Trade Center and its history.

After that, we were walking on the streets of NYC. There Scarlett and Laura took over our company and didn't say anything about what they needed because everyone was in a good mood but we all made a really good bond that day. The next day Scarlett and Laura joined us for all our activities. The next day in New Jersey, we went on a tour of the statue of liberty. It was the most exciting thing ever done. First, we got tickets for the cruise ride then we followed all way. Peter, Louis, Laura, Scarlett and I were taking so many pictures I don't know where but I hated to take pictures of myself but that day I took so many.

We had so much fun. We then reached the museum. There were many audio options to listen to about the history but I went with English. I saw many tourists around. It was a great time listening to the great history of this statue of liberty.

Then we got back on a cruise and had a closer look at the statue it was so huge and amazing. I never had experienced sometime like this before. It made me fall in love with some. My friends and brother were enjoying it too.

Next, we stopped at a food court of course after everything we were a lot hungry. We grabbed some food. Had lunch and an amazing conversation. We even got to know Laura and Scarlett very well.

" So Kevin, did you like this tour? " Laura asked
" It was one of the best things, trust me. "
" I am glad you liked it. " Louis said
" What about you Louis and Peter? I enjoyed as Kevin did." Scarlett asked
" Me, it was best, I would love to come to the USA again. "

" Me too. " Louis said.

" Kevin, when are you going to California?

" Tomorrow, but I am nervous. I never met them and suddenly. I will panic. "

" Don't worry it's will be alright you guys are friends. " Scarlett said. I nodded but I still feared.

We left for the hotel and it was nearly twilight shining in the sky and it went dark after all the busy day all of us got tired. So we went and took a nap and that nap was so long we did not get up till morning.

The next day was a good start. Today was a day to cover some more of the history of New York. We went to a lot of museums and historical places.

We were supposed to go to some more spots but I decided to go to California first then join them later.

8

I went to the airport by 9 pm. I got checked in and waited till I am aborted. I was traveling alone which was a big deal for me. I don't travel alone. So I thought instead of going there all by myself I got my brother along with me. I hope they don't mind it.

They gave an announcement that the place is about is take off. I got this, I can do it. I know it was not a big deal but for me it is. I grabbed my brother's hand because I know I know I did not have the courage.

It was so long I thought. I read a story on the flight where else everyone was sleeping. After some time I fell asleep too. When it was time to get down. I noticed I was sleeping over Louis.

I got off him and said " It's aching? "
" What's aching? "
" Your shoulders where I took the nap"
" It's ok don't worry. Did you change the time? "
" Yes, I did. "

We got out of a a plane in some time. " It was 5 hours flight can you believe it? "
" Yes from Toronto it was nearly 2 hours."
" Yes," I said

We went and stayed at uncle's house whom we ever met for years. My mom said to go to his so we did it was weird that we started there with his wife and two little kids but they were really cute.

One day later Harvé and Cassey decided to meet at a restaurant. I finally was going to meet them.

When I reached there. I was not able to find out who was who. Later Harvé made a call and he said he is wearing a hoodie and t-shirts. I noticed he was just in front of me. I started to panic. My heartbeat increased, I started sweating my legs started shaking and I lost my voice.
Harvé started coming near to me.
He said " Hey Kevin, So nice to see you! "
"Yes, you too" How to say it out Louis was staring at me the whole time. " Kevin come on you were waiting for this all the time. "
Cassy came there from back and gaveHarvé a big hug. She looked at me and said " Kevin? Anything wrong? "

I finally got the courage to say it " Yes, Hi Harvé, Cassy finally we met together. " My voice trembled but it's ok.
" Kevin doesn't get nervous or stressed, it's ok. " Harvé said to me it did feel better but then he got me in his arms. "Long time buddy " He laughed and said, " Long time it's like we met already ".
I felt better, it was ok I was not nervous anymore " Yes, I think we did meet. Three of us. I forgot to mention this is my brother Louis. "
" Hi, Louis. " Both said.
" I got him cause I am scared of flights. "
" It's fine, I am too Cassy said. "
" You too! "
" Yes, " She replied. I felt it was not just me there are more people who are scared of many things doesn't make me weak or nerd.

We went to a restaurant. We ordered some food and till we got our the food we talked about so many things like. How we talked online and finally are talking to each other in person. It was so great. I hope I could have them forever but it's ok I know sometimes we can't have what we want.

Casey's food came first. It's the most awkward moment we face. We asked her to start but she didn't till ours arrived too. When we got our food on the table our conversation gave an amazing taste. It was just a joke I used.

Then we all went for a walk. Got ice cream and enjoyed it all over everything. We went shopping. Harvé and I got a dress for Cassy. It was beautiful on her. Of course, it could be she looked gorgeous in it. Cassey is like my little sister and I love the way she is. Both of them were as sweet as they were online. Nothing changed. Of course, the day didn't go the way I thought but it went much better than I thought. It was best of best.

Then we went back to NYC. It was time to say goodbye I felt bad. I wanted some time with them but I only asked for a week and it was over.
" Bye guys, I said to Harvé and Cassy. " They came to drop me till the airport.
" Bye, gonna miss ya. " They hugged. " Yes me too. "
" Have a good trip, bye Louis. " Harvé said

We went back, it was again a long trip. It made me so tired.

When we went back we had some plans to do but I got sick so we did not leave the hotel. So Louis decided that he will stay with me. This is how we spent our last days in the USA. I was in bed for the whole day and only took some pills. It only made me feel a little better.

By the time we had to leave I was better. Then we took our flight to Toronto. When we reached the airport we saw mom was waiting there. We ran towards her and grabbed her in our arms.

" How was your trip. " She asked
" Best " We both yelled.
" That's good. "

Then we left for home. We talked a lot about our days in the USA. We talked and talked a lot. Best trip ever!

9
Burst out

I am still not happy with Scarlett's and Laura's idea of bursting into Margaret's house. It was not a good thing and even I have a sense of bad feelings. We were outside looking for a good moment to go inside. While I started speaking
" Are you guys sure we should be doing this?"

Laura
" If not then why are we here? "

Louis
" Don't worry bro, it will be fine "

I said
" What if we get caught, someone sees us. Even it's the afternoon we aren't doing it at midnight. Anyone can see us. I will warn you guys again we shouldn't be doing this. It's a crime! "

Scarlett (getting mad at me)
" What if….what if. I will kick you from here or push you from a cliff into the water of the Caribbean Sea? What ifs in your head isn't reality, reality is never what your think, it's something more than those shits in your head. You can never think, everything that's gonna happen, you can never. So stop thinking things and discouraging yourself. Prove them all idiots wrong whoever said you a looser, brat, coward and everything they say bad about you. You have something in you proves it. Even we get caught no one's gonna send us to cops. "

I said
" What if they do…… ".

Peter
" Kevin seriously? "

Scarlet getting more frustrated with me
" You will stop for a second. If anyone sees us we will escape. That's why you are here to freak out? If you have so many problems then go, we will get help from Louis "

Louis was looking at me and of course, I don't want to leave him alone.
" Ok, sorry. I won't utter anything anymore sorry "

" Better " Scarlet said. She continued " It's a good time, let's go in "

Laura
" From where? "

Scarlet
" From door want to enter in? Of course from the window, I found out to be opened "

Louis
" Ok "
" Good kiddo " Scarlet

Scarlet was in lead and we were following her. I was at last. It felt so different. I was never in such a situation before. I don't know what was coming further. It was adventurous.

Suddenly I noticed scarlet struggling to open the window so I asked " What's wrong? "
" It's not opening " She replied

" But you said it's open. What to do now? "

Scarlet
" I will find a way. Don't worry. Wait " She started thinking. " Let's break it "

Laura
" Are you kidding? Anyone can see us doing that, what if anyone hears it? "

Peter and me
" Yes, I agree with Laura ","Same here"

Louis was at the other window and said from there " No need to break anything, look it's open"

Laura
" You did not check which one was open Scarlet? Good work kid (to Louis) " She started laughing looking at Scarlet.

We jumped in, it rarely been a month and it was as dusty as an old woman's house who as left that house decades before she moved to Alaska. Do my words make sense?

It was dark inside and nothing was working in there. So we turned on our phone's flashlight and started moving.

Peter
" Where do we have to go? "

Scarlet
" To Margaret's room, top left corner "

Everyone started moving upstairs. Scarlet was lost and doesn't seem alright so I asked " Are you ok? " She " Yes…. Yes, nothing's wrong."

I said, " Ok, let's go".

When we reached upstairs we came across some creepy things and the worst thing behold was spiders, it was everywhere, what can be good to them rather than an abundant house. It was annoying me. Scarlet pointed out toward a door and said it's Margaret's room. " Was," Louis said. "Ok was or whatever," she said. She tried to open the door and it was locked again. She was frustrated with things and said "Agggg…. It's lock what the hell should we do? "

I said " Don't loose your temper just brake it "
Scarlett" Brake it? You are crazy? "
"No I said to break your anger" and opened the door she was doing it in the wrong direction. She eventually got mad at herself for acting stupid from the very start.

When We entered the room we were damned. There was nothing inside. It was all empty. We stood there staring at that empty room and were like " Scarlet it was not what you said? " There's nothing inside? "

Scarlet " Sorry, I am so sorry. I was stupid enough to think of it. So sorry "

All of us one by one " It's ok, don't feel bad ", " Yes, at least we tried ", " Yes you said right, we shouldn't be sad about things we can't control ". " It's all right, scarlet ". She started weeping. Laura got her and tried to make her feel better and suddenly Louis shouted
"Mom's coming " Everyone started looking outside. We should leave because she or anyone can't see us this way. I don't understand why we're here. Everyone started

stepping down. Louis rushed so he can divert mom from seeing us. While going down I found some pieces of paper and I grabbed them and started looking at them. Peter yelled " What's wrong with you? Quick ". Yes, I replied and started hurrying up.

Louis jumped off the window and crossed the fence making sure he can reach before mom sees him. He was standing there and started pretending as nothing happened. Peter was wondering if he might mess it up. We were watching Louis from across the street.

Mom saw him standing outside. When she took a step out of her car. She asked Louis
" Who are you waiting for? "
" Your mom "
" Really? " She asked
" Ye... Yes"
" You're ok? You don't seem alright? Do you want something? "
" No, I don't want anything " Louis replied
" So where is your brother? " Mom asked
" He is chilling out with his friends "
" Friends! " She was confirmed because I don't go out with anyone and stay home. I even don't have any best friends to chill out with.

Louis and mom proceed to go inside we thought it could be good to leave this place before I get any attack because of the thousands of thoughts in my head.

Mom suddenly turned back. Is something wrong? She started wondering. Louis turns her attention towards him and hopefully, they were out of sight.

Peter
" What's wrong with your brother? Why is he acting weird?
"

" What are we still doing this? "
Peter hits me and says " Again! "

Scarlet
" Move, move we can go in now, you know what to say to
your mom right? "
" Yes"

Laura notices the papers in my hand
" What's in your hand? Where did you get it "

Scarlet
" Move we can talk about it later "

We were out of that place my heartbeat again was so high.
We thought no one saw us but it was a kid looking at us
from his House's window. Although I did not notice him.
It will be a massive change if he comes in.

Peter rang the doorbell and mom opened it. She was
surprised to see Peter because he usually doesn't come
home
Peter said " Hello Mrs. Watson "
" Hello Peter "
Scarlet and Laura followed Peter and said the same. Mom
has never heard of them so she said " Hello, I am sorry. I
fear I don't know about you both. "

Scarlet said
" Oh yes, we are new friends of Kevin. I am Scarlet and
she is Laura. " Mom was still in confusion. Well, it was

hard for her to believe things. " Ok then, have a good time "

" Thank you so much. "

We were all going to my room which was upstairs. Before we could mom called out to me and said " Kevin, listen. It was quite surprising but I am proud of you honey. That you are getting social and making friends and going out of your room, really "

" Yes, mom " That's what I can say the best because I don't know what to say. I wasn't socializing or making friends, I was just helping them and later they will be nothing.

Amy was thinking
"Kevin is finally making friends, suddenly after the USA trip, I find a little change in him. Yet I am scared, what if he is hurt like he got last time. I don't want him to be sad. I can't stop worrying. Ah! Help him. "

We were in our room Peter started cracking "Honey I am so proud of you that you are socializing " I was quite embarrassed but it wasn't hurting. Louis " Don't make fun of mom".
Peter
" No no, I was making fun of your brother because this guy is finally socializing and I know your mom always wanted it " (He cracked again. Scarlet and Laura also started laughing along)
Scarlet
" Hey, Kevin are you that bad? Don't make friends and go out? "
" Yes," Yes I replied.

Peter

" Traitor, I am not your friend? I hate you! " He got mad

" No, please don't take it in the wrong way "

Peter

" Wrong way? I will take it in the wrong way.

" Sorry " He wasn't serious so he started laughing. He scared me.

Scarlet began

" Sorry guys, because of me you all have to…. To do everything, sorry "

I said " Come on don't be sorry. Even I was a little scared honestly a lot but it most amazing day of my life. I never did something so crazy before "

Scarlet

" But we did not find anything and I ended up being a stupid "

" I have found something " Showing those papers I got earlier.

Scarlet " What! You did, Ahh! Better than nothing "

" Yes and don't feel stupid. You did it for your friend and I am sure is watching from somewhere and must be feeling lucky to have you. Even you are so amazing if you look inside you. You have all the beautiful views. "

Scarlet

" Thank you so much. You know I feel so bad that I

wasn't there for her, in her last days. Even if she killed herself, why can't help her? Why? I always feel so responsible. " (she felt really bad.)

I said

" It was not your fault, it will never be. You know, you sometimes don't want to kill yourself but want to destroy that part of you and it gets so hard to get rid of it that you give up and end up with the worst things, she is safe where ever she is, I am sure she doesn't have to go through the pain there that she faced here. Even she would never wish you to be sad about anything. "

Scarlet
" Thank you so much, I feel a little better."

Peter
" It's hard to understand Kevin. He can motivate anyone except himself. "

Louis
" My brother is weird "
(yes said Laura and all started laughing) .

I said
" So here, I got some papers. I think it is some sort of motivational speeches and writings Believe in yourself by Dr. Joseph Murphy, Ikigai, how to win friends and influence people by Dale Carnegie, Anthony robbins awaken the giant within and that's it"

Laura
" Was she trying to motivate herself? "

" I think, this one's, I guess she wrote it "

Scarlet
" What! "

" Wait I will readout
You are something amazing

You shouldn't think too much about what people will think of you and be insecure about every single thing. You are great and you always will be. No one can change that. Care for no one's word because they make no place in your life and never will.
If people ever crisis…. Sorry…… Criticize you just forget it and think of yourself because they will never make any place. Don't even care about all the scoldings it's alright. Don't criticize yourself too even more. You might get mad easily but handle it with a smile. Your works are always amazing. Not for others but for you it should always be because you are only doing it for yourself and nobody else. Don't Care if people share, comment, or like your post because it's not at all important. Most importantly stop hating yourself because you are the most lovable person and that star which is gonna shine the brightest in the sky…." (that's it)

"Your friend was on social media too? And works she mentioned here. What does she use to do? "

Scarlett
" She wasn't. Actually, we never talked about it and the work you asked about. She use to write. Write articles. "

Laura
" If she use to then why she would commit suicide. I mean

she writes and reads many of them. Motivational speeches and articles why she would? "

I said
" Sometimes these things don't work. No matter how much you try you still have that feeling that kill you from inside. You….you feel hated by yourselves for being alive. Having anxiety is more than overthinking and sad feelings "

Peter
" You can understand it better right? "

I said Yes because I understand. I was suddenly having a weird feeling in me. That I can't express. I guess I will break into pieces again.

10
Richard

My name is Richard Kanye….. I am a bad husband who always fights with his wife. I have two sons and I think I have failed to be a father too.

Speaking about my childhood, it was the worst one, I was the youngest child to my parents, my siblings were 15 and 17 years older and you can imagine the gap. My mom passed away because of lung cancer when I was 6. My dad soon became an Alcoholic and most of the time he comes home drunk. My brother soon became an alcoholic too in his early 20s. I hated alcoholics. I started hating them too. Soon my dad died of liver cancer, he had it hidden for a long. I have to do everything all alone because my siblings refused to help me out with them. I had suffered a lot and

I don't want Kevin and Louis to suffer the same. So sometimes I am strict with them but they would ever understand? I had no one to guide me back then, so I have gone on the wrong way, did things I shouldn't have. What can I do now, try my best so my sons don't either? Why they don't understand?

Now I run a business that my closet friend handed over to me before leaving this world. I took over all his business because he had no one to take care of it and he trusted me the most. You can understand how hard it would be handling everything, especially it's so stressful, the whole of the business. Most of the weekends I fail to be with my family and they get mad at me. Don't I feel bad? Don't I? That I cannot be with them enjoy my time but rather I will be in my office getting annoyed. I want to be happier too, I want my days back when I have everything. I don't have to handle this work and spend my time with family going out on weekends, trips, holidays, everything but once lost time cannot be back and reality is my sons hate me now. They don't want me to be home. My wife Amy doesn't like me anymore either. Thinking of them brings me back to the day we first met had Kevin then Louis, Ah! Those days can make me cry…..

Flashback

I clearly remember the 24th of July 1997
I was sent to a person named Amy Watson and when I first saw her my heart fluttered. She was so beautiful that I can't stop looking at her. She was wearing a red shirt and I clearly don't remember what happened at the back because I did not care about anything but it was only Amy. Ah!

Such a wonderful and passionate woman she was. She still is, I don't doubt that.... I was so lost in her that I didn't notice how amazing she was drawing. I thought if I don't go and talk to her then I can never. So I went to her and asked

"Mam, your work is really beautiful, how does it come? "

.... Our way conversations went on and I noticed that she had such a pure soul.

Back then I use to draw too so I helped her out drawing those campaign posters. That's what Amy said. Talking of her voice, it was so sweet as honey and I loved it once I heard it. I wished she didn't stop speaking. I asked her thousands of questions and she answered them all and I got fascinated by her. They were so many of them I could speak of and all do memories in my heart. I would carry it forever.

The best of it was in Venice. It was the 15 of April, we were on the tour of Europe and Venice was our last spot, of course, I was having a surprise for Amy. First, we started a walk nearly at 6:30 am down to Ponte di Rialto, the oldest bridge over the Grand Canal in Venice. Then we stayed there for 2 hours. Yes, 2 because we enjoyed looking at people and enjoyed the atmosphere. Then we went on to Libreria Acqua Alta is a bit off the beaten path in a quiet area where not many tourists are seen. In this crazily decorated bookstore, they sell secondhand books, postcards, maps, and calendars. There are books everywhere you look, even in a huge gondola and bathtub that's inside the bookstore. We got some postcards, maps, and some amazing calendars. Then we decided to enjoy the streets of Venice. People said there are many busy streets in Venice and getting lost in them will be a fun experience stroll along the canals, cross bridges, locals enjoying their coffee moment and see the real beauty of this incredible city. Without a doubt one of the best things to do in Venice. We had a good time together. We went miles long holding hand in hand. Then at last at sunset, I started getting nervous and my heartbeat was at its peak, finally the time as come. I was scared. We took a Gondola ride in Venice, a unique and romantic way to see Venice is by cruising its canals with a gondola, but the only thing I thought was of Amy. Sun was over the horizon and then the sunset was matching the water flow. The Colour of the sky matched my feelings with the same feelings I fo p but was more nervous and tense. Millions of questions in my head, I slowly bent down and open that box, box of my love, my life which was about to be with her, with the person I ever loved the most one I want to be my wife, my better half. Yes I asked

"Will you marry me? ". She was shocked for a moment and then started crying, happy tears. She said screaming " Yes and forever Yes". Ahh, best day and I could never forget in my life. I started crying too. Yes, I was emotional.

About the ring? She did not notice all the time? It was with my friend who has given me before the Gondola ride..... "

End of flashback.

But now the only thing I do is fight with my wife. Of course, she doesn't like me anymore. Whenever I come home my children don't want to see my face. Ah! My life. That day when I came back Amy, Kevin, and Louis was done eating. I want to spend some time with them at least have dinner together. I was sad and a little frustrated which was all thrown away on my wife and we fought. I was all stuck with my work but she was right, I was late and how can I expect them not to be all stuffed by now? I am really stupid. I want to apologize for whatever I ever did. I left in anger but I went to my office and cried out all the time, I was hopeless.

My kids hate me so much that they don't want to talk to me or even ask for my permit? Or at least say me anything? Kevin and Louis were going on a trip to the USA, none of them said anything. Even I came into knowledge a week before they could leave.

I AM NOT A GOOD DAD, A HUSBAND, OR ANYTHING. I HAVE FAILED TO KEEP ALL THE RELATIONSHIPS, I AM USELESS..... I AM NOT A GOOD PERSON ANYMORE. HOW DO I BECOME SO SELFISH WITH TIME?

I wish I can get back to that day again. So beautiful they were. Rather I can never get them back, once time gone can never be back. I should have enjoyed those fruits, it's not late yet I can get those days back. I can quit my job and start taking care of my family. Although who am I doing it for? Them why they don't understand, everything I do is for no one else but them. I want them to have the most comfortable life that I ever had. I would never wish them to go through the same what I did. Still, I wish I can have a happy time with them so they can start loving me.....

11

A DAY AFTER

My trip was over, I was back in Toronto It was fun but now I feel so alone and depressed, being with people was never my type and now I feel so stupid of myself that I tried to socialize. Each and everything I did was coming into my head. I don't think of good stuff that happened back on the trip but all the embarrassing moment was bringing thunderstorms. It was not many moments but I was creating them. Like why did I say it? Why? When no one was hearing it? I was never heard then why do I need to speak up? Or I should have said it in a better way, was I mean to them? Everything was so annoying! I was better alone Why did I ever try making new friends when I know I will end up increasing my anxiety(I hit my hand on my forehead in frustration). No, it was not their fault, they have nothing to do with my anxiety, it was just me who is introverted. I know many people find it difficult to adjust with me. Ah! So amazing was quarantine, I know it cost a lot but still better for an introvert like me. I will give my words an end now.

I was feeling weird to come back online, I have said to them I will be back in 2 and a half months but it's already been longer. USA trip, exams and other things I did, it's been 3 months and I don't know how to face them all. I feel that I have to go back and I can't. There's a reason, I met them because of fandom, I loved them and I found many people who liked them too, a year later I lost my interest in them, I don't like them anymore and I know how crazy is fandom toward people like me, not all but some. I don't want them to say bad about me or judge me in the wrong way. I was thinking all of this and then suddenly I thought of Margret. (It's 5 am and thoughts burst in, I can't fall asleep, it's always hard to fall asleep when my sleep break before the start of the day). Just wondering why she would do everything? I mean whatever Scarlet thought is it necessary to be true? I want to know the truth, after all, I was thinking to take the same step, I don't think it's worth it anymore. I still have those papers I got yesterday. I have them under my bed, just in case.

I went to grab them, it was a mess, all the paper. No doubt that I am a clumsy person. I started reading everything again but more carefully, she use to read motivating books and note them down, so she can read them again and again till she feel better. " I hope there was a day she could love to be alive" That's what comes to my brain, I should know the real reason, I want to. I did not notice when I fell asleep again, it was 7 am and Louis was shouting at me to wake up, of course, it was getting late but I don't want to wake up, I wasn't able to sleep earlier. " Ok," I said 10mins later and rushed to get ready. Almost by 8 am,m I was done eating breakfast so I can go out of here. Who would like to go to school, such a dump place? No, not every time only when I get ridiculous comments from people or it's a freaking shitty day.

I would walk down the hallway. Who would enter the class when the last one's chemistry. God! Take me out of here. It's not just me all my classmates hate the class or are scared of the teacher, I think. I was walking straight seeing at an angle of 90°, yes I got dashed at someone and then my dumb ass want to freak out. I started " So.... Sor... Sorryyy... Sorry, I wasn't seeing and I dashed into you, I don't mean it please forgive me ". He said," Dude chill why so scared? I won't rip your ass for just getting bumped into me, come on". He left raising his hands upwards. Like why? Again I did something wrong. My behavior will never change. I stepped into my class and I got the last seat in the corner, I hope they don't have an eye on me.

Someone turned back to me and said " Did you read it? Please don't remind her about our test" I was ... " What! What test"

" Great, "she said" You don't know she asked us to read both the chapters for the test? " Shit!! Did she just say! I am dead! I did not read! Then Mrs. Bethany our beloved chemistry teacher entered. (I use beloved in a sense of anger). She was like " Ok so I hope you are ready before I can take a test I will ask a few questions ". She was looking everywhere to ask that freaking question which was on her head and then her eyeballs fixed towards me my heart was about to pop out in nervousness, then she called out the person right in front of me, Ah! Hopefully, it wasn't me, I was quite chilled out by that. Ok, misunderstanding happens. She asked a question and I was like " Dude I read it, even I forgot I have a test I do remember everything I read ". I whispered the answer to myself but it was quite loud that the person in front of me heard it. It seems she didn't know anything and repeated what I said and Bullshit! It was correct! She then looked and smiled. Mrs. Bethany looked at me and pointed out to me " Whoever you are at the back, say me...... " She asked me the bloody question and I was totally out of my mind by now, I knew the answer but I did not say it, was I gone crazy? I was ready to take punishment but I wasn't to say that answer. Then as expected she got totally mad at me but her kind heart left me, but to be honest I would have took punishment,I deserved it .

After the class some bullies comes to me " You little brat, last time I asked you, you had no answer and again today you did not have any! "(last time! They still remember? It's been 2months or more! Move on) " You! I thought you could have some character development after that but no I was a fool to think so, you scored well this time right, in your examination? What do you do? cheated? Because I don't think you study anything. " After all those words and after getting embarrassed in front of the whole people in hallway I opened my mouth and answered. To them defined got more mad at me " You..... (there wanted to say something but controlled there language, After All, it's school)..... You know what you have no future if you do the fucking same. Ever thought what are you gonna do? If you did, I would love to say you, you are never gonna succeed in anything, you will be in the most rotten place in Canada in the worst apartment, jobless and begging for a living because I don't think you will have much more than that. No one's gonna give a job to rodent-like you. Ever looked at yourself? You are just a little piece of shit no one's gonna look at. Even no one's gonna split at your face. You are a disgrace to your parents, your brother is a million times better than you ever thought of that? No one ever loves you in this world. Your parents will be embarrassed to have a son like you" I was completely embarrassed. You would ever say that? Anyone on earth would say a student like that? They are no one to decide my future. No one. I am breaking inside now. They looked at me and yelled again "you are still here? Get out of my here. I Don't want just students here. Get out! " They yelled at there maximum voice. I was completely still there, I can't move in embarrassment " Get out before I threw you out of the school" I started packing and left. I was outside the hallway and then I cannot control myself from crying before I could reach the washroom. I lay down against the wall and started crying like crazy. Outside the hallways was empty. Scarlet and Laura appeared from nowhere. Saw me crying and was beside me, one of there's hands was on me, I didn't notice who's. Laura said " What's wrong? " I cannot say anything even if I try my voice wasn't coming out. Soon the class was over there was a bell given out. It was the last class of the day and I can go home now. Before anyone could see me crying I ran out at the earliest. Scarlet and Laura tried to chase me but I was out of their sight. Peter approached from the back. "He ran away". "We need to find him". Laura and Scarlet look at him and asked " What happened? ". He has recorded everything that happened in class after seeing the clip both of them was, of course, mad at her behavior and said: " How Mrs. Bethany can do it? It's completely ridiculous, he is already going through anxiety and other many things and she is doing this ".

Scarlet, Laura, and Peter rushed to my house and Louis opened the door. He wasn't expecting to see them. I wasn't home yet.

He asked after they enquired about me
" Who? Kevin? He isn't home yet" Louis
"Where did he go? " Laura
" What happened?" Louis
" I want to talk to him, he left from school crying he had a bad day today, really scared " Scarlet
" Wait what! I want to come with you" Louis

" But where " Peter
" I know where he is " Louis

Louis took everyone to a place. It is quite quiet There was a little pond where there were some scattered trees all around. Soft grass layed down and not many people were around. Kevin was sitting there. Hopefully, he was here!

"Kevin " Said Louis
I looked back. All of them came to see me. Does anyone even care for me?
I shouted " Go! Leave me alone, I don't want anyone " I wanted them but I don't know how to face them anymore.

Louis took no more second and sat beside me so did scarlet, Peter and Laura did.
Peter " I know you do "
I started speaking " Aren't you guys embarrassed to have me as a friend? Louis to have a brother like me? I am just an ugly piece of shit. Who is useless. "
" Dare say any more word I will rip you" Laura
" How can't I? I am tired of everything I want to live no more, I don't want to live. I am just a disgraceful son, brother, friend, and everything " I started crying again

" No! No, you aren't," Louis said and I can see tears in his eyes " You are the best brother in this world and I am so lucky to have you "

I said " Speak no more good of me Louis. You were always there for me whenever I needed you. At last, what I just did, I just yelled at you because I was anxious about some things. I always regret that. You have been the best, not me. I could never help you out with things because I am a total mess. I have been the most useless big brother. I have so many reasons not to be alive, I just don't want to live anymore. I don't regret my decision of ending my life, anymore. I am done "

(wait! Did I just! Just said it. Louis was looking at me surprised and that feeling I can never explain. All of them were looking at me. I know I need to say them everything but I can't explain anything anymore).
12
Louis was looking at me so was everyone. There was an awkward silence. Then Louis started. I wanted to leave so I got up. Louis yelled
" Dare move a bit. What do you think it's all joke to you? You don't love us anymore? Say me. Do you? If you care then you would not think of it. You remember whenever dad gets panic attacks or gets stressed it made us all tense. Didn't it? Then how can you think ending your life won't affect us all? Mom and dad will mentally die. What do you think? I can't live without you, Kevin. I can't! I know I am younger but still... Why don't you understand? I don't want to lose the best brother in this universe. You are worth everything, you are so much to me. You.......you can speak. Speak to someone. Not me than anyone? We will get you out of here. Ending life isn't a solution, not at all. You are precious, treasured, everything, a gift to us. Kevin! " Tears started falling off his eyes, so was from mine.

Scarlet began " He is right Kevin. It will affect all of our lives, not just one. You are our friend. We all love you and trust me you are not alone in this fight. We are always there for you. You are the best person I have ever met.

Kind, helpful, and cheerful, the life of our group. You can't do this. I have lost one friend, not again"

I started again " I know, I know but try to understand I am tried, tried of trying to be happy. Fighting to live every day. I can't handle my pain anymore. I can't"

Peter gets closer to me " How long has it's been? "

I replied " 3 months ago I wrote the note "

Laura " You ever wrote the....! What! "

(I didn't expect my truth to come up this way! I have to speak the truth. Will they understand? I don't know how to explain)

Laura silently said " Ok, don't freak out, come sit let's sit down "

I said in guilt" Sorry guys, I made you all mad. Isn't it? "

" We aren't mad, we can't express what we feel right now, but trust me, we are not" Laura

Louis cutting in between " I am though "
Scarlet gives him a stare. We all sat down and Peter said " Ok, take a deep breath and say us all your problems. We promise we won't judge or get mad at you ".

I looked at Louis he said " Yes, we won't "

"But Kevin we might try to solve it but we aren't experts, try to get better help. Talk to your parents. "

"I know I should, I don't know how to explain them. They are always sad because of my previous behavior and regarding my health issue, how they will take this one? Even they think a kid like me doesn't have any problems and should always be happy, how! How! Can I? "

" Think, they are tensed about little things of you? If you just quit your life doesn't that gonna affect them completely? " Scarlet

" Yes... But how are they gonna understand? " I can't control myself, I was going through a breakdown and it usually lasts longer for me.

" Understanding, that's the problem. No one understands each other, no one wants to understand anyone, anyone's problems. Not just because sometimes they don't want to keep their weapons down and talk to get a solution, No! " Scarlet

"Are you ok? " Laura to scarlet

" Ye... Yes"

" You are sure? " I asked

" Yes, don't worry," She said

" Tears in your eyes does not define that you are ok," I said

" I have gone through the same, what you are Kevin. Just circumstances were different. Sorry, I don't want to make this about me, we should talk to you. Sorry " She swipes the tears.

" No, no Scarlet, it's just not about me. You are here to make me feel better. It's being selfish if it's just about me. All of our feelings equally matter "

" I know but speaking about you, where did you write the note "
(She went out of the map)

"I__ I wrote it in a hidden app. So no one sees it "

Peter " Kevin! Seriously! "

" Ok, Peter doesn't get mad. Continue Kevin " Laura

I started "It feels like, it's never gonna end. My feelings, my....my insecurity, anxiety, overthinking. I can never get out of this condition, especially overthinking about certain things cause I do it for so long. How can I end it so easily? When nothing positive happens in my life, how can I speak of something positive? When I am such a negative speaker, anything I say or think doesn't come true then, how can I? It's so troublesome. There's no way out, there's nothing. Sometimes when I see my parents comparing me with other kids who are doing better than me, I want to end my life or I wish I wasn't their kid because they deserve a better son".

School just pressurizing into things to be better, to be perfect or I make no place in this world. How can I? You saw right Bethany said was, I have no future, right? I can't do anything with my life. What's the use of keeping it? "

Peter " Kevin there's always a way, there will be a way through this too. Nothing lasts forever, your anxiety, your sadness will end one day too. Just you need to realize and trust in yourself. If you don't think you can make it through you can never. If you don't work on yourself no forces on this planet can help you. "

Scarlet " Mrs. Bethany, did or said was bull shit, who are you listing to? A shitty person cannot decide your future never! They make no place in your life. They will never. You know how annoying it becomes if you keep her stupid unreal words in your heart. Just let it go because she is no one in this world to you. No one. She is just a wave she will go away."

" Right, I shouldn't and stop caring about things. I should let things so. I will not think of it again, I promise but what if some people doing the same is inseparable. "

Louis " Who are you speaking of? "

" Mom and dad. Sorry but sometimes you know.... "

Louise "I know what are you speaking of"

" It's not like they don't love me they say it for me. But they never say me in a good way and demotivate me a lot. I know they care for my future but they yell at me for not coming up to their expectations, which is so depressing sometimes. Being an elder son, I am not like how I should be according to them. I am not worth a 17-year-old teenager. Sometimes they just say I am like a first-grade student and it hurts. Which is shit. Even they say I have no future. How can I handle everything! "

Louis " But you know they never mean it"

" I know but you won't understand. You are their favorite kid, you are good at everything, you don't understand what I have to go through! They just fight with each other. Throw each other's frustration on me and then at the same time they are so good to you. "

Louis " What do you mean! You think I don't get yelled at, I don't get scolded! Or you are just blind enough to just see your problems? Kevin, you have the same problem you don't see someone else's problems too"

" Ok, really Louis? Thank you but you are good at everything, get everything you are wishing for what you think of yourself? Huh? "

Laura " Stop! Stop for a Damm second! Stop! (there was silence) ok, stop fighting with each other on pointless issues. You think fighting will help?"

"It's endless honestly, sorry "

" Sorry, Kevin " Louis

" You know how it's like having a sibling and losing them! You do? " Scarlett

" What happened Scarlett? "

Scarlet" Nothing "

Laura " Are you ok, you never said about it. "

" No Kevin, you are going through a lot. I don't want to speak about my past and everything..... And yes Laura I didn't mention it. "

" You know, if you speak, I will know it's just not me and I will get a sense of hope that I can do it too. "

" Yes, but won't it be selfish? "

" No, it's not. "

Scarlet " Ok, I was actually. I don't know where to start... I was 4 years old, I was the only kid to my parents and I always have seen them fighting since. I have never seen them happy, caring for each other, or even have seen them having a sense of love. They only fought and blamed each other for everything and finally, they decided to leave... They got divorced, you know how it is like when you have to decide who to live with. I loved them both equally, I have to finally be with one. I saw them fighting for my custody. Soon my choice did not matter no one asked me what I want. I know I was just a kid and cannot understand what they were going through but there was no one with me. Anyone to come and ask. My life! Soon judge passed his mission. My mom got it but decided I could stay with my dad two days a week. Which was mostly weekends. I use to have a good time with him but I always missed my mom when I was with dad and I missed dad when I was with mom. It was so annoying but soon I noticed my dad did not care about picking me up every weekend. He soon stopped spending time with me and even took me out, he did not even call me. He even didn't pay a visit, for months together. I would always ask my mom, I know she had no answer. She finally talked to dad about this. He just said that he was busy, busy with his new family. Within a year or so he got married again, got kids. I eventually became invisible to him. He did not care for me anymore, he only spend time with his family. Like we never existed

I was scared that how I lost my dad, I would lose my mom too. I didn't want that. If she leaves me I will have no one in this world, no family, no parents, no one I will not have anyone who loved me. She promised me she will never leave, my dad promised the se thing earlier, didn't he leave? I believed in no one's words anymore.

I hated his daughter, he was not my dad anymore. He left us when we needed him or I did. I think he left because he already had his girlfriend and was seeking a moment to leave us. Circumstances bring you to a moment where you have to do things you never wished to. So I was with his daughter in a social group. Her name was Emily. She was my sister, I know that but I didn't want to work with her. I requested my mom to leave the group but she did not listen to me. Soon I need to accept her and eventually, we became friends. She never knew I was her sister.

So one fine day our group decided to go on a hike. It was going well every time was fine till Emily's foot struck a stone and she slipped down into a 12,000 feet cliff. You know what would have happened.

So we all came back, I was terrified. He came in and saw me and started yelling. He blames me for everything that happened. I was already having a bad time on her death and he was the one blaming me. I did nothing, nothing! My mom was with me. She took a stand against everything that happened there, she went against my dad. We decided to leave the country and we moved here. It has been years since I have seen my dad. Losing Emily was the most painful experience in my life after all she was my sister.

Then Margret only person I can rely on. She was the first person I first met here, eventually my best friend. When she said me she is suffering from lung cancer, I know I will lose her some or the other day. She... She was slowly recovering from her condition. Then suddenly, I get the news! (she started crying)..... Sometimes I feel I am the trouble maker, it's Always because of me people lose their life, family, love, I am the cause of all problems. My parent's relationship got bitter when I was born and then their separation. I lost my sister because of some reason and I was there. I lost everything because of it. I even lost Margret because I came in. Or at least I feel bad for not being there for her, she didn't say me but I should understand she needed me, I was with her still I was dumb enough to not understand her. Such a bad person I am. I don't know why? I know she didn't die of sickness, that night when she left, I went to sleep earlier than usual, I regret doing so. She was trying to reach me, she was texting me, trying to call me but I did not hear anything. If I took some time and answered her call, she might be still here. It's the greatest guilt of my life. "(she was still crying).

Laura " Sorry, sweetheart, I am sorry you have to go through all this but it's none of your faults. It happened and it was not in your hand, nothing was. You can't blame yourself for things that were destined to be. You are the best, you take out people from their worst problems, you are not the trouble maker, trust me. I know it's helpless, anyone in your will have the guilt of doing so. Please don't cry. It's not your fault "

Scarlet " But I fear, I will get close to you guys, I will lose you too"

Louis " True Scarlet, it's not of your fault. Don't think, please. We won't go anywhere, I promise nothing bad is gonna happen, ok."

" Right scarlet," I said

" True we are all here for you, we won't leave you ".

" Thank you "scarlet.....

13.
You know me already, I am Louis Watson Kenny. A few days ago as you all know, my brother, Kevin said he was planning to end his life and I got mad at it, of course, it was annoying when your brother just suddenly reveal his feelings he was hiding for a long. I knew he was going through anxiety but I never imagined he was about to do something like this.

He is the best brother on this planet, so kind caring, and always here for me. Why does he think he is useless? Why does he think I am doing best not he? I am a good brother not him? I have so many questions in my head. I know his brain is making him think so. Why he takes little things so perso, all,y I wonder. He can't let things go easily. I have seen him thinking of things that happen 10 years ago, yes! Someone stop him from doing it.

How to say him he means a lot to me, a lot and I can never get over it if he takes any bad step. How to say him? Mom and Dad will they? Will they be happy after then? I know like Scarlett's they will blame each other for everything. I can't imagine any further. It's gonna hurt more than anything on this planet.

Why does he think I have no problems? Do I have to not go through anyone? Why? Mom and dad's fight, doesn't it hurt me as much as it does to him? Why is he going blind? Sometimes I feel he is like dad, he won't want to understand things. They have had had so much in common. There's always something you love in someone and something you hate. If you love them you try to ignore that bad side but if that bad side is just a lot then the concern you can never see the good one. My family has so much concern for each other but they never do it. I don't know when we were all given a big hug and said " I love you", I don't remember. They are hilariously shy to show love or concern, it's so annoying when you openings yell, scold or shout at anyone but don't want to show love to them, why?

I have seen my parents yelling a lot at Kevin, I feel really bad for him, they always scold him for not coming up to their expectations, demotivate him so much. Even tell him he is worthless, it's not away, it's not. But truly speaking he is suffering a lot than I am. But his blindfold should understand my life isn't full of fruits and I am enjoying them. No, I have things.

Well, last Christmas I speak of the worst thing I have ever experienced in my entire life. I was begging my mom to get me a new pc, it was not working properly. I know I have to do that. I was asking her for the last 6 months. Finally, I thought she could give me one on Christmas. Guess what... I was so excited to open my gift but it was just a bunch of books and Kevin got what I was begging for the whole of half year! Damm! Why?

I remember how worst was Christmas when dad yelled at us (Kevin and me) saying " You both stop acting this way. Do you think you are sick, both of you? You know kids don't have a mental illness. If you want to, I will take you to the hospital tomorrow then you can see real dying children. You both make no place here to think of it. " It did not hurt me a lot but Kevin it did. I have no mental issues, he does. I wish I can say to them to stop and think of him a little, can't they? Didn't they have problems when they were younger? Why don't they see?

I was sitting in my room, I suddenly started thinking of Kevin. I went to check on him. He was not in his room, I just started walking around till I noticed a piece of paper lying on the ground, it say......

"Does my name even matter anymore?
Or it's just a form of the word someone else chose to give me,
It's just gonna carve on the marvel stone
after I end my life,
No one's gonna use it again because any memories of mine are just going to be forgotten on a blurry night when I wasn't there.
They will have the concern for a week,
They will moran for a day or two then everything will be

the same, like how it used to be,
I will have no one visiting my place,
My name will slowly disappear and I will matter no more here.
Because no one cared if I was even there.

I know I might be writing this but I never wish my parents and my brother one day to wake up just to see me lying dead on the doorstep of my room".

What not again, what am I looking at? Oh god! Kevin. My heartbeat suddenly started rising, he wasn't around. Hell! Did he. No.....no I can't be thinking of it. No! I want to see Kevin right now!
Where is he?

Sadly I hear a voice "Louis " Relief it was Kevin. He was standing at the end of doorstep He asked, " What are you doing? ".

" I - I was looking for you and I found this__"

" You what? "

He sees the paper in my hand and grabs it from me, " You were reading this? "

" Kevin, listen. I care for you. I can't see you suffering, you know since you said about your feelings I can't stop thinking. I fear, I fear to see you leave. No matter where I am ambulance's noise always makes me trill that something has happened to you ".

I can do nothing but give him a big hug.

Kevin " You know I don't want you to worry about me, it hurts. "

" It hurts, even more, to see you suffer ".

I noticed something on his hand " What's that Kevin? "

" Nothing," He said. I can't ignore it
" What that, tell the truth "

" It's nothing "

I yelled, " Stop lying Kevin, say me the truth ".

" You want to hear the truth right? I have done it, I have cut my hand. Do you want to hear anything else? "

" Why? Why do you do this to yourself? Kevin, you need to get help "

" Take help? So they can say it to our parents and then to everyone. So they can know that I am a psycho? Wait Louis you think the same isn't it? "

" Kevin no, wait, Kevin! " (he left)

What should I do? What, I can't stop myself from crying. I tried speaking to Peter, I gave him a call.

Peter said not to worry a lot about it, he will get him out of it. I wish I can do something better but will he hear me?
I hope Peter gets him out.

I am scared every second I am scared, that I might lose somebody, I might lose my mom or dad or Kevin. It stresses me a lot. I can't handle things anymore. I fear the next day I wake up with bad news of somebody close to me, somebody I loved the most, somebody who was mine.

I remember the day when we went swimming in the ocean, it was all good till a huge wave came in and it almost drowned me in. I since then started getting scared of high tides and waterfalls for some reason.
Once there was a neighbor's house burning into ashes I remember. I started getting scared of fire too. I know many things hurt me not and the most are death or losing somebody close.

(Next day)

Kevin was sitting in the class he was 20 minutes earlier. He was just sitting around and he gets a comment from a random boy from somewhere.
" They you go, am I looking at a coward who was pushed out of chemistry class? "

He can't handle words, he is way too sensitive to handle critics. He left the place and they said again " Look at this coward again running away. "

He was in the washroom. He has done something terrible. The tissue from which he was covering his hand was filled with blood and Peter was standing there " Is this the solution of their words? "

" What are you doing here? Did Louis send you here? " Kevin yelled

" No, he didn't, I was stalking you, anything you want to say in your defense? Because I won't let you ruin your life like this, you get it, Kevin? "

" No, you are no one to control my life. "

" I am your friend and even if you don't take me as your friend then I don't care, I do and I can't let my friend hurt himself terribly, you get it. "

"Fine what you will do? Say, my parents? Ask me to go to a council? No, I won't let you do that, everyone will know. "

" Why do you care for their words Kevin? They make no place in your life. "

" So do you, go away from my life. "

" Ok__ ok Kevin, I will go but I won't leave you because I know you need me. Sorry. "

(Peter leaves, Kevin was standing there holding his hand. He trashed the tissue and left) .

Peter talking to Scarlet

"What! What is he thinking? What does he think of himself? ".

" Why is he doing this? There must be some reason? "

" Some reason, you mean anxiety? I know he has anxiety but he doesn't get a free card to hurt someone or himself especially. Who will say to him he is precious and amazing. Who will say him? "

" He got mad at me and left. Someone should say to him people can love such a kind soul like home. Why won't he understand? "

Kevin comes appearing from there and sat down and began " Sorry guys, I am so sorry Peter, I love you guys, and yelling at you made me feel so much guilt. All the time. Sorry Peter ".

" Don't apologize to me, what you said I am no one, then why did you come to a no one? "

" Sorry Peter, I didn't want to really. "

" Ok, don't repeat that. One more thing stops apologizing to me and thinking you were not harming us hiu were harming yourself. Whenever you do so it hurts a lot. Why don't you understand? Please promise I need you will never do that again and if you break it, I will never trust you on loving yourself. "

" I promise I will never do that. I know Louis was worried too. I will try my best to avoid it but trust me. It takes time. " (Kevin started crying)

" Since then when you been doing that? "

" Since two months. Whenever I feel down, I wish to cut down each piece of myself. I know I deserve more of the pain I give to myself "

Scarlett " Kevin, Kevin no you don't, trust me you don't at all deserve that. You deserve to be happy not to get yourself hurt. You don't deserve the treatment you give to yourself. Really. "

" I don't scarlet, I don't ".

" What you need to realize that we love you, that people care for you? "

" Nothing I just need a break from this world from the thunderstorms. I want the light, blooming flowers. I am tired of hearing about all the family fights, now I fear to have any in the future because I think I will end up like my parents."

Peter takes a deep breath " Kevin no please don't. You are amazing and don't fear. Which family doesn't have fights? You can't hurt yourself by proving yourself responsible for everything. "

" Right " Kevin started crying even more.

" I am a crap Peter, I am. I don't want to get judged, I don't want anyone to hate me for taking that step, and for a once I don't want to do it. My family can't live without me. "

" Come here Kevin," Scarlett said. Peter and Scarlett gave him a warm hug

Everyone wants somebody with them in their hard times. Someone who can speak to them and understand them. Someone who can love them through their fight with themselves. Till they make it. Anyone who doesn't judge them for their actions and takes them of out it. Someone who makes the person realize they are the most precious person on this planet alive. They are not worthless, they are not misfits. Please stop saying things to people which might hurt them. You might not realize what they are going through, what they are fighting with, and how much your words can affect that person. If you can't help anyone please don't make it worse.

14.

(Kevin)

It was finally the 24th of December I was having a good time, of course, I have holidays but it felt so good, I don't know why I wish this Christmas don't get ruined like last time. Please! no!

I was helping up with things, cleanings, getting the Christmas tree ready for tomorrow, etc...

I wish I don't have a bad Christmas or any one of us like last year when everything messed up, my dad yell at everyone especially me, since then the only fantasy which comes inside my head is having cancer of death so my parents can understand that I am suffering. So grief, pain, and loss sometimes so people and notice me and I can have people around me caring. I know there are many people out there suffering from all of them and it's so painful to them, but I can't stop thinking of those. I wish I can give my soul to a person who wants to live. Every time I take a selfie, I feel how ugly I am and I hate myself even more. I feel insecure every time I see myself. Either in pictures or a mirror. I would love to hit so hard so the mirror breaks into pieces and my hand bleed militia's the last drop. Then I even feel bad for not being in the picture. I think it's better to not take a picture than take all the insecurities.

(Amy)

I wish this year's Christmas is a good one, I wish. I am not gonna mess up with the gifts again like last year's

Well, the cabinet was left to get cleaned up. I know it was just a day left for Christmas and still, the cabinet was dirty. Kevin and Louis helped a lot in cleaning, I don't want to make them busy, I will let them enjoy their time. Even I don't know why I want to do it all by myself. I went upstairs and opened the freaking cabinet and Damm's dusty stuff started falling of making all my clothes untidy. I went down to pick them up. I found something, some old memories I don't want to look forward to. No, not memories of mine and Richard but my childhood. A bad one, I sat now stretching my legs. I started going through them. I chuckled at the picture of my brother and mine. It was cute, I miss him, it's not like I don't meet him but we have no good relationship anymore. We don't talk anymore, we don't call each other or even have uttered words lately. But I have called them for a family get-together tomorrow. Yes, it's only because I am close to my sister-in-law, and Kevin have a good bonding with his cousin, it is obvious because both were born on the same day. It was a coincidence a good one.

I wish I can have my brother back, I can talk to him but I am scared, scared to make a call and say to him, I still love him, I still care. I wish I can say him tomorrow that I want him to be my brother again but I don't know-how. Long lost happiness is never gonna come back. I have a lot of regrets but it's not gonna bring anything back.

I started going through the pictures again. It was an old family picture of mom, dad, and my brother. I remember making an imaginary story of our space war, far away in the galaxy in our cardboard spaceship, haha. I remember everything. I don't have to take over any responsibilities, have no stress, I don't have anything to be sad about. Life was perfect, even not when I lost my mother at the age of 13, I lost everything. My dad never said me the real reason for her passing away, I wish I can get her back. She was sweet kind, amazing, and a really good mother. I wish I can be like her but I know I have failed to be one, I am nothing like her, I am not good, I am not good to my kids sometimes and fail to understand them.

I stared at the pictures for the next 40 minutes and it all reminded me of good and bad memories but mostly good ones. I pay nothing for it. I am grateful for having some good memories rather than those sad presents.

I was looking at them, I was almost crying till Louis came in and said " Mom are you ok? "

" Yes honey, are you fine? "

Louis
" I am fine but I don't think you are, may I help you out mom? "

" Sure if you can, thank you. "

" Mom, anytime. ".

He helped me out with the mess, we dusted everything out got all the things arranged properly, and done. Finally, the cabinet was clean before the end of the day.

I saw Kevin passing by I haven't seen him the whole day do I asked
" Are you free now? Where were you the whole day? "

" No mom, I have some work ".

He was smiling at me, I know he has not much work
" Ok, so what do you have to do? "

" Well, I am busy, I have to go to Spain. "

I laughed at his answer " What you will do in Spain?"

" Eat Olives "

I cannot stop laughing at his answer
" Olives? Kevin? You can give me a better excuse ".

" Yes, what can I do? " He cracked

" Check if everything is at the right places for tomorrow. "

" Nah," He says no but he does the work.

(Richard)

I am not gonna work tomorrow, after all, it's Christmas and I have given leave to all my employees but do I have any left? No, I think but I don't want to disappoint my family or make them sad. I always do that. I am scared, I might ruin their day.

I am going home and I don't want to because I always end up having fights and they even don't understand me.

(Kevin)

It's time for bed and my brain isn't letting me sleep. I can't stop thinking. So many things are bothering me, like after school, death (I don't know but yes), Louis, Peter, Scarlett, Laura. I don't know I can't cease thinking of them, especially tomorrow, what will happen tomorrow? What if it messes up? What if there's a fight again? What if I become a problem with something again? What if there's no end to things? What if... So many things were bringing thunderstorms.

Scarlett said, " What ifs aren't reality which I create in my head, it's what's happening and I can't always have control over it. ".

I was thinking of all this and I finally slept. Hopefully, I did.

MY LIFE SUCKS!!!
15.
I am at the seashore watching the tides hit the cliff with the force of everything, the retreating waves. I was looking down into the deepest of water bodies. It was overcast, It felt like something bad is gonna happen soon. I made my step ready and made my last run jumping into the blue water covering a very vast area. I was drowning and drowning the light was disappearing slowly, it was getting dark and I was losing my soul.

I got a sudden jerk, I opened my eyes, I was on the bed. It was just a dream! It scared me. Was it a sign? Sign of having a bad Christmas this year?

I should stop overthinking and freshen up. I rubbed my face against my hand and got out of bed but I didn't wish to.

I went inside and looked at myself in the mirror took my hand through my brown hair and was thinking, how ugly do I look! Why can't I be better? Ok, fine everyone is beautiful, no one is born perfect.

I was done taking a shower, I put on some new clothes and went downstairs and my mom comes hugging me said "Merry Christmas, Kevin "

I said " Merry Christmas mom". Hugging her

"So how your day started, good? "

" Yup," I said. Well, Yes, I lied about having a good start. Louis came from another way to wish me. Dad was there too.

" Everything is ok? Merry Christmas everyone, love you all. " My dad said it and it was quite surprising for me.

" Merry Christmas Dad, love ya. " Louis and I said. " Merry Christmas honey ".

" So what should we do today till your cousin come over? "

" Bake a cake together," " Good and Kevin what you wanna do."

" Me – I wanna go out for a walk with you. "

It was the best Christmas I ever had we went got shopping, got some candies, had lunch in our favorite restaurant. Then we got home by 3 pm. We all backed a large chocolate cake together and then decorated it so beautifully. I think we never had this time together in years. My mom was happy, Louis was happy, dad was happy. I was happy. Everything was perfect.

Our cousins came over, My uncle, aunt, and their two kids were over. We had a peaceful dinner, everyone had a good conversation until our uncle mentioned what his big son is doing these days. He said, " Mark got selected as the national football team captain." Immediately my dad said, " my older son does nothing, I don't know what he is gonna do in the future."

" Dad, please don't say that, I know I can do something, and it's better than being a stupid captain of a stupid team."

" You can't speak to your cousin like that, apologize to your cousin, Now!"

" I shouldn't, you should to me. Why never do you think of us, what we did, and everything we can do? You never encourage anyone for being who we are rather than comparing us. Have you ever known what Louis and I are good at, never, never! "

" Thank You so much for the dinner Amy, I guess we should leave." said my aunt.

" Stop, Stop " my mom yelled. " Sit down, I said sit down, now. " I got scared from her tone of speech.

" You all just keep fighting, ever anyone of you thought what is going through me– what I am going through? No, nobody can understand the pain of a mother. You were never told that when you become a mother each part of you goes to your children, you break and break, till you are into million pieces and that broken pieces of you are never gonna come back to you, never. Everybody cares what they go through what they want but anytime any of you thought what your mom, your wife, your sister goes through or when through? You know what you need to stay strong no matter what's happy in your life because for your children you are not just a person you are their hero and they think heroes never cry but you know what they do when they are completely broken, they do." She started to cry.

" Mom, please don't cry, I am sorry," Louis said and started crying. He went to her and hugged her " sorry mom ".

" Mom it's all my fault, I have been selfish all the time, I did not realize that you also go through a lot. I am sorry." I said

"It's not your fault, Louis, Kevin. I always love you and you will never be the problem. I – I just got emotional sorry."

Mom " All fault is mine. I never know. What is happening in Louis, Dad and your life. It triggered me always that ho much hard times I have, I always talked about what is happening in my life , how my anxiety is affecting me I forgot it's not just me but my world but everyone!

"No honey, it's not your– " My Dad yelled cutting Enough that's from not what me in between you expect your family, one just have to how much she sacrificed say as mom, one doesn't know what he is doing , a dad is doing, other just don't care what is happening with Others and just think about themselves .You don't Amy, ever thought why I never get time for you and spend with our kids? Ever you tried to know what happened with me and my life in these 15 years. No!".

I left in that mood. My mom stood there crying. I cannot control too. I went upstairs and locked myself in the room. Louis was just sitting and crying at the dinner table. Our cousins and their parents were sitting there, when they saw my father leave, they went confused about what to do there when they my left out . My mom was standing there to do something then, she shouted "Wait,Wait" for Richard,she went back of my father trying to catch him

She saw him getting into the car. She immediately got on the other side on his and opened . She took the door and tho side You Ok ". My dad asked "What are you doing here Amy, please leave"

My mom said in confidence." I am not leaving you " He started what car and started to drive somewhere.

"Where are you going?", my mom asked. " I am not saying," My dad replied " I am going to travel where you go then. "stay" My father yelled. ever Leave My Mom want me trusted him, so she kept both and " If you trust me then let me go where I am going." My dad said, she replied "Never I won't. If you or you of course disbelieve you, I trust you." h

Meanwhile at home. My Aunt Stop was making Louis comfortable " Don't cry honey, everything will be ok. " He said " Our family is breaking apart . Nothing is gonna be what it was before. "

"Don't cry Louis, we are here . We talk to your parents" here we will

It as my fault I was crying . Everything always will my fault! I have been Selfish all the time. I started weeping and sat down against the door . Time I started so hard and harder why, why I even everything,why am I here? here. I am a problem. I should end it. I end it today. I went downstairs, in the kitchen. Slowly into the kitchen and saw my antidepressants and all my asthma pills. taking all of them one by one and by.

I don't remember I took that day. how many of that

When I opened my eyes hands were plugged in. I had all put in . I noticed on oxygen support and I was in the hospital. I don't know what was going on. What happened ? What happened?

16.

Some mon was Standing near me well I can barely see through my blurry vision I saw my mom, then Dad "Kevin," both cried out In their lower voice.

"Hi,". I said to them "You are ok? " dad asked "Yes, Dad I am fine"
"Sweetie, why do you do this?" Ma asked in tears

Mom, I just thought I was being a burden on you both. I was good for nothing and I was just a dis dishonor -

"Kevin, how can you– You are our Son. How can you even think that? You know how much happiness you brought to us. You became the whole world when you were born. You were everything to us, then Louis came. We all became the world to each other. You know. will be the most hurtful losing any of you"

"Lessen our discussion of all We cannot live without each other"

You are our whole life, it will be destroyed. understood it? In all-time)" Mom Dad said it together

"I thought you got fights, anger in the family because of me and I thought we were drifting apart "

"Kevin" (Louis came to me. His hand was in mine and he was crying we in "Hold a while , you understand"

Importance of anything. our family Never-never "I want to know But know apart what happened before How did I come here"

the

Louis ,"Kevin When you started in those pills talking from the cabinet I went to the kitchen. and I to found lying on the ground and the pills were around you . Uncle was there, he called out called and our parents. I got scared the moment I saw you . Aunt and Uncles got you to hospital . Doctors said If it went a little late we would have lost you." Louis holds my hand tighter

-crying and grabbed my "Sorry Louis I am so Sorry"

'I should be so sorry, it my fault you know what it's not your, all are my faults not yours"

fault it's just ... I don't know

Previously...

My Dad was driving and reached a place
" You remember this place, Amy. "
" Of course how can I forget about it. "
" We had a really good time together. "
" Richard you remember whenever we wanted a break we always came here. To have some time together"
" Yes, I guess today is a day too because we need a break,"
" You are right we need to come. "

They both sat down on the grass and started looking at the stars in the sky.

" Wow, it's beautiful, like you Amy. "
" You said it on our first date. " She looked at him and smiled.
" I don't know what happened to us in these days we got mad at each other. Everything. "
" It's my fault too, I never tried understanding you either Amy. "
" How about a good new start where we give time to each other maybe even some here sometimes. Kevin and Louis are old enough now. " He gave a big smile to her.
" Always, Richard. "
" My life is all that's yours, Kevin's and Louis'. I thought I need to do my job just to support my family. I was wrong, I need love too. I was thinking to sell my company and spend some time with you all, with my family. I know Amy

you can handle everything else. I cannot do anything without you so "

" I appreciate your decision. I always thought that your friend's business slowly drifted you apart from us. "

" Yes it did but the most important thing is we are here together forget about what happened, a new beginning is waiting ahead. " They were holding each other's hand and looked up at the sky.

Suddenly my mom's phone rings
" Who is it? " My dad asked. " It's my brother Harry. "

" Yes, Wait what. No – it, where. I am coming " My was got worried when she got the call.
" What happened Amy. "
" Kevin he tried doing something he was found near the medicine cabinet lying. We need to do to the hospital quickly. "
My dad went quickly to the car. They hurried up.
" Why this all took place today. " My dad was crying out.
" Yes, yea what have we done. "
" Right, " He said in worry.
He stopped the car parked it at the earliest and got up to the place where I was lying unconsciously.
" Oh, god " My mom cried
" Is he ok? " My dad said to Harry.
" He is quite serious. "
" Mom " Louis cried and grabbed my mom, Kevin will be ok mom? "
" He will don't worry we are together," My dad said.
"Yes, your dad's right. "
They all waited till they heard anything from the doctor.
They were the whole time sitting there.

" He is fine now. "
" Thank God, " My mom said.
Louis started weeping again. " Can we meet him? "Dad questioned
" After he gets up " " Ok "

I said in the hospital for rest a week, I had all the tests. I went in for medical counseling, metal checks up, and everything. It was weird. I got so many get-well-soon cards, especially from my most amazing friends Laura, Scarlett, and Peter. Out of all I never had felt so close to my family before they were with me as much as the time they can. Even Louis didn't want to leave but he have to, so did my mom with him. The most beautiful part was dad always stayed with me and I had the best bond with him in those few days than I ever made in years.
I found out how good a singer he was, a good artist he was and he even said the secret that my mom taught him to draw that good, even I saw how caring loving amazing person he wasoverallll I saw the most amazing dad in him.

Finally, I came back home it was 31st of Dec. Last day of the year. Louis and mom came to pick me up. Dad was there too. When I reached home three of my friends were standing there. I screamed in happiness " Laura! Scarlett! Peter! " I went and hugged the three. " Louis what are you looking at come," said Laura. He ran towards us and given that big, giant hug.

" Thank you so many guys for coming over and checking on me," I said.
" We would just leave you, they didn't let us in when you are in but we sent all cards, flowers, letters"

" Yes I saw them. Thank you so many guys, for everything.
"

" Forever. "

We went inside into my room. Scarlett said, " How dare you take that step, I didn't say you earlier I didn't want to lose you or any of 'em. You know especially you. " I saw drops of tears in her eyes and all she wanted to say was that she suffered when I was in.
Before I could say anything she kissed me. It felt so light as feathers. When she left me everyone said " Oooo". " Guys stop," I said and started laughing.

" You know Kevin we were finding what happened to Margret? It happened what we thought and you know what. Tomorrow is a new year. I want you and us to get a new start. We are thinking, we can start an online website as a way to help people out there who are going through hard things and to tell them how important they are to some people so close in their life. Their kids, partners, friends everyone. " Laura said

" Yes, not just for Kevin, Margret but for everyone. "

" You are right, for everyone. " I said. I hugged them again. " Love you guys. "
" Love you too. "

17

It was summer we all went for a vacation. I and my friends were standing on the seashore by the cliff. We were holding each other's hands.
" Here we are. A time where you all were apart, separate

but now we are not anymore. " Said, Scarlett

" We have each other, our family, our friends, and mostly each other. " I said

" Let all the worries go away in this tide and goes not let it come back like the sea touching the shoreline again and again " Louis

" For everyone, we had, for everyone we lived till now let's forget that and live for ourselves and forget about all the things that made you worried. " Laura

" It's gonna take time, less or more we don't know. We don't know how many days it's gonna take. There are a lot of obstacles waiting for us in our ways, let's promise not to give up in any circumstances and not leave each other and hold on this way forever. " Ricard

" If anyone falls we will pick them up. We found the best of each other and the worst but that doesn't mean we are gonna let go of our friendship our love, easily. "

I guess the woes were not the special thing that happened today. The special thing is what happens every day. My friends, my family, my love, and myself, my true self.

We were having lunch together my parents and my friends. I am 18 now. I see my father not being disappointed by me because I changed. My mom does worry about me because I changed and my brother does did not crcryecause of me, cause I changed. Everyone changes. Everyone does. So did I and now if I feel lonely I know there is someone to hold my shoulder and say " Don't worry, I am here."

We don't know what's coming in the future but I am ready to not give up and move towards better.

~~~~~
~~~~~